For my parents,
the first Mr. and Mrs. Green

BOOK ONE

Meet

Mr. and Mrs. Green

KEITH BAKER

Harcourt, Inc.

Orlando Austin New York San Diego Toronto London

www.HarcourtBooks.com

First published in 2002

The Library of Congress has cataloged an earlier edition as follows:
Baker, Keith, 1953–
Meet Mr. and Mrs. Green/Keith Baker.
p. cm.
Summary: A loving alligator couple enjoys themselves as
they go camping, eat pancakes, and visit the fair.
[1. Alligators—Fiction.] I. Title.
PZ7.B17427Me 2002
[E]—dc21 2001001955
ISBN 0-15-204954-1
ISBN 0-15-204955-X pb

A C E G H F D B
A C E G H F D B (pb)

Printed in Singapore

Contents

Camping

It was Saturday morning.

It was sunny, and it was hot.

"Let's go camping,"

said Mrs. Green.

Mr. Green had never
been camping.
He was excited.
Life with Mrs. Green
was full of adventure.

"We need a tent," said Mrs. Green.

"A big tent!" said Mr. Green.

"With lots of room."

"We need sleeping bags,"
said Mrs. Green.

"We need food and water,"
said Mrs. Green.

"We need warm clothes,"
said Mrs. Green.

"And pillows!"
said Mr. Green.
"Soft and fluffy pillows."

"Like chocolate bars
and marshmallows,"
said Mr. Green.
"And soda pop!"

"And bunny slippers!"
said Mr. Green.

Mrs. Green continued checking her list.

"We need a camp stove.

We need boots.

We need a first-aid kit.

We need flashlights.

We need matches.

We need hats.

We need a harmonica." (Mr. Green was a musician.)

"We need paints and paper." (Mrs. Green was an artist.)

"And . . . we need a map."

"A map?" asked Mr. Green.

"We need a map?"

"Yes, this map," said Mrs. Green.

"I made it last night."

Mr. Green began to worry.
We're going far away,
he thought.
There could be
dark, mysterious woods,
strange, eerie sounds,

spooky, glowing eyes,

sharp, pointy teeth,

and mosquitoes!

Mr. Green was not excited anymore.

He was scared.

And he hated mosquitoes.

But Mrs. Green wasn't scared.

She was ready to go.

Mr. and Mrs. Green hiked over their
welcome mat and down their front steps,

past Mr. Marble's rock garden
and his barking dog, Boulder,

beside their favorite picnic spot

(where Mr. Green once ate six watermelons),

across Polliwog Bridge

(the best fishing spot in town),

around every pothole and
dandelion in Shortcut Alley,

and through a squeaky back gate that
looked (and sounded) very familiar.

Mrs. Green pulled out her map.

"We will camp here," she said,
"next to the birdbath."

Mr. Green looked closely at the map.

He saw the path they had just traveled.

It ended at their backyard—

their cozy, comfortable, beautiful backyard.

Mr. Green was excited again.

The grass around the birdbath

was thick and soft.

It was the perfect place

to set up their tent.

He would sleep like a salamander.

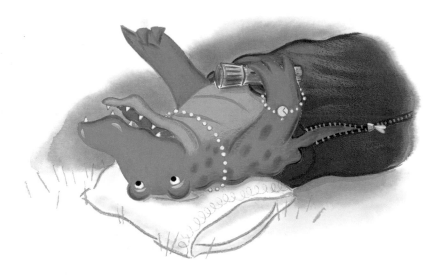

After dinner they crawled into their sleeping bags.

"Look at that moon!" said Mrs. Green.

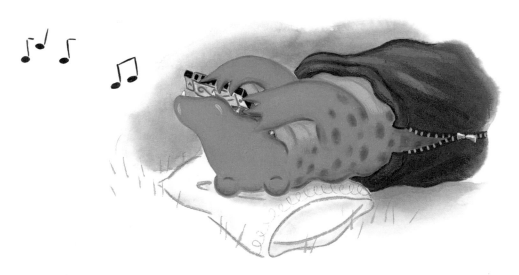

"It's like a giant marshmallow," said Mr. Green.

He began to play his harmonica.

But he fell asleep before finishing even one song.

Mrs. Green felt happy.

The sleeping bag was snuggly,

the stars were twinkling,

the frogs were croaking.

And best of all, Mr. Green

was snoring loudly by her side.

100 Pancakes

"I'm hungry," said Mr. Green,
"for pancakes!"

He licked his lips.

Mr. Green had not eaten since

his midnight snack.

Mr. Green loved to eat.

(His three favorite meals were breakfast,
lunch, and dinner.)

He loved to eat pancakes most of all.

"This morning I could eat 100 pancakes—
fat, flat, and round!"

Mrs. Green was surprised.

(Life with Mr. Green was full of surprises.)

"Did you say 100?" she asked.

She knew Mr. Green could eat a lot.

Once, at the movies, he ate 22 tubs of popcorn.

But could he eat 100 pancakes?

"One-zero-zero," said Mr. Green.

"10 times 10,

50 plus 50,

349 minus 237, divided by 2, plus 44 equals—

one hundred!"

(Mr. Green also loved numbers.)

"With butter and syrup?" asked Mrs. Green.

"Yes, please!" said Mr. Green.

"And rainbow sprinkles."

"Okay!" said Mrs. Green.

She began to count. "1 . . . 2 . . . 3 . . . "

And Mr. Green began to eat.

And eat,   and eat,

and eat,   and eat.

"Only one more to go—,"

said Mrs. Green,

"and it's a beauty!"

"Stop!" said Mr. Green.

"I am full,

I am stuffed,

I am packed with pancakes.

I . . . can't . . . eat . . .

any . . . more.

It was not like Mr. Green to quit.

He needed some encouragement.

Mrs. Green had an idea.

She turned away from Mr. Green.

Very carefully she cut the last pancake
into the shape of a star.

"Try this," said Mrs. Green.
"It's something new—a starcake!
Each point is a tasty triangle,
and the center is a perfectly
scrumptious polygon.

Delicious with butter, syrup,
and rainbow sprinkles."

Mr. Green took a little nibble.

He chewed.

He swallowed.

He smiled.

"Yum," he said.

"Heavenly.

More syrup,

please."

He popped the starcake
into his mouth,
and it was gone
in one big gulp.

"You did it!" said Mrs. Green.

"That makes 100!

A starcake *is* a pancake.

Let's celebrate—

with chocolate cake and ice cream."

Mr. Green said, "I could eat one hundred and *one* slices of chocolate cake with—"

He stopped. He rubbed his round, full belly.

Mr. Green looked . . . *green*.

"I'll just eat one slice of
chocolate cake now," he said.

"And save the others for after lunch."

County

50

"It's time for the fair," said Mrs. Green.

"And you know what that means!"

Mr. Green began guessing.

"Ring toss?"

(He loved the ring toss,

especially when he won.)

"Ferris wheel?"

   (He loved the Ferris wheel,
   especially being at the very top.)

         "Snow cones?"

            (He loved snow cones,
            especially red-cherry snow cones.)

"Yes, yes, yes," said Mrs. Green. "And more!
Think about judges . . . and prizes . . .
and big satin ribbons."

"Oh!" said Mr. Green. "Your paintings!"

"And your flowers!" said Mrs. Green.

"Let's try to win first-place blue ribbons this year."

Mr. and Mrs. Green hurried home.

It was always fun to be part of the fair.

Mrs. Green took out
her paints.
"A splatter of red . . .
a plop of yellow . . .
a drip of orange . . . ,"
she said.

"A smear of purple . . .
a wiggle of white . . .
a smudge of pink . . .

and green!
Apple green,
lime green,
screaming green—
and turquoise!"

(Green was Mrs. Green's favorite color.
Except for ribbons—she liked blue.)

"That," said Mr. Green,

"is a first-place painting!"

Mr. Green went out
to his garden.
"Blooms of red . . .
clusters of yellow . . .
petals of orange . . . ,"
he said.

"Blossoms of purple . . .
buds of white . . .
posies of pink . . .

and green!
Olive green,
mint green,
shamrock green—
and chartreuse!"

(Green was Mr. Green's favorite color.
Except for snow cones—he liked red.)

"That," said Mrs. Green,
"is a blue-ribbon bouquet!"
Mr. Green stuck the extra flowers
onto Mrs. Green's hat.

On the way back to the fair,

Mrs. Green held her painting tightly.

She was thinking about

blue ribbons.

Mr. Green was thinking about snow cones.

When they arrived, Mr. Green's vase was empty.

"Oh dear," said Mrs. Green.

"Oh my," said Mr. Green.

His flowers wouldn't win a ribbon this year.

But there were still
the ring toss,

the Ferris wheel,

and slurpy, slushy
red-cherry snow cones.

And Mrs. Green's painting could win a ribbon.
Mr. Green grabbed her hand,
and they walked into the judge's tent.

The judge looked closely.

"The red," he said, "is radiant!

The yellow—yummy!

The orange—outstanding!

The purple—pleasing!

The white—wonderful!

The pink—perfect!"

"And the greens—
all grand and glorious!
Sennnnsational!"

The judge pinned a blue ribbon
on Mrs. Green's hat.
"These are fabulous first-place
flowers!" he said.
(Mrs. Green had forgotten about
the flowers on her hat.)

"And your painting," said the judge,

"is a marvelous mountain masterpiece!"

He placed a blue ribbon

on Mrs. Green's painting.

Now she had not one but two blue ribbons—
two big, beautiful, very blue ribbons.

She turned to Mr. Green.

"This blue ribbon," she said, "belongs to you."

Mr. Green felt dizzy—happy dizzy,

Ferris wheel dizzy.

"Ready for a snow cone?" asked Mrs. Green.

Mr. Green did not answer.

He was admiring his blue ribbon.

"READY FOR A SNOW CONE?"

Mr. Green came back to earth.

"I have another idea," he said,

and he led Mrs. Green to the Ferris wheel.

At the very top, they snuggled close.

"This," said Mr. Green, "is better than

a blue ribbon."

"Better than a red-cherry snow cone?"
asked Mrs. Green.
"Hmmm . . . ," said Mr. Green,
"I will have to think
about that."

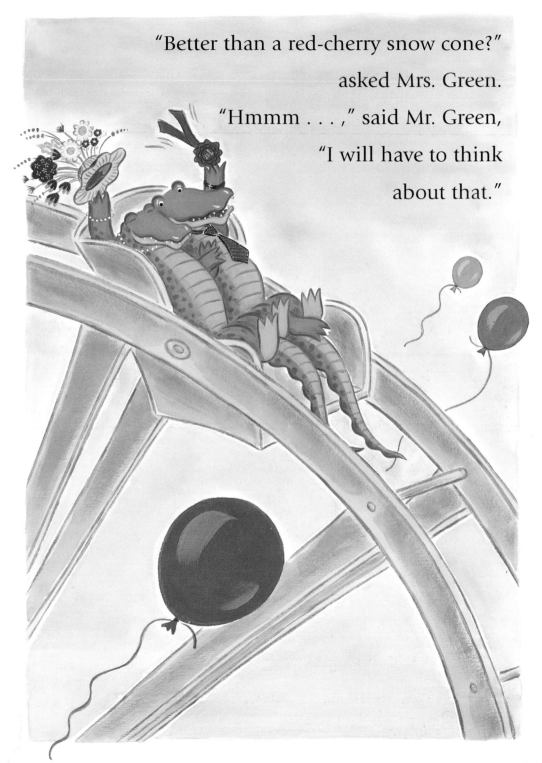

The illustrations in this book were done with acrylic paint on illustration board.

The display type was created by Jane Dill Design.

The text type was set in Giovanni Book.

Color separations by Colourscan Co. Pte. Ltd., Singapore

Printed and bound by Tien Wah Press, Singapore

This book was printed on totally chlorine-free Stora Enso Matte paper.

Production supervision by Sandra Grebenar and Ginger Boyer

Designed by Keith Baker and Team Green